I0390092

# The RUNAWAY PANCAKE

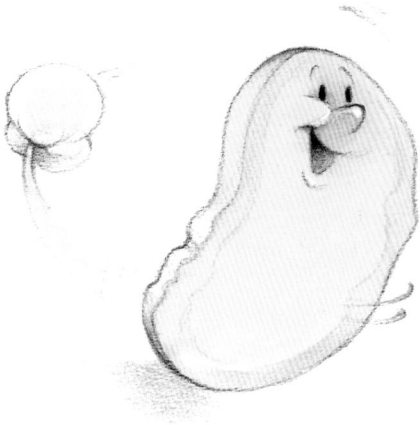

Retold by
Mairi Mackinnon

Illustrated by
Silvia Provantini

Reading Consultant: Alison Kelly
Roehampton University

There was once a family
with seven children, and
they were always hungry.

One day, their mother decided to make pancakes for breakfast.

First she mixed
flour, eggs and milk.

Then she poured the mix into a pan to cook. She tossed the first pancake, up in the air and down again.

But the pancake didn't want to be eaten. It jumped right out of the pan and rolled out of the door.

"Stop!" cried the mother.

"Come back!" called the children and they all went running after it.

The pancake rolled out of the gate and into the road, faster and faster.

The dog was snoozing in his kennel when the pancake rolled past.

"You look good,"
he barked.

"Come here
and let me taste you."

"No!" said the pancake and rolled on, with the dog and all the family chasing behind.

A rabbit in a field saw the pancake rolling past.

"How fast you roll!" he said. "Can I catch you?"

"No, no!" said the pancake and rolled on, with the rabbit, the dog and all the family chasing behind.

Hee, hee, hee, you can't stop me!

A duck on the stream saw the pancake rolling past.

"Stop, Mr. Pancake!" she called. "Just let me try a tiny piece of you."

"No, no, no!" said the
pancake and rolled on,
with the duck, the rabbit,

the dog and all the family
chasing behind.

A cat in the farmyard
saw the pancake roll past.

"Stop! Wait for me!"
she called.

"Catch me if you can,"
said the pancake and rolled
on, with the cat, the duck,
the rabbit, the dog and all
the family chasing behind.

I'm delicious but you'll never catch me!

A goat in a meadow saw
the pancake roll past.

"What a
fine-looking
pancake," he said.
"Do you taste as good
as you look?"

"Of course!" said the
pancake and rolled on...

with the goat, the cat, the duck, the rabbit, the dog and all the family chasing behind.

A fox in some bushes saw
the pancake rolling past.

"Oh, Mr. Pancake," he said. "Why is everyone chasing you? What have you done?"

"Can't stop
now," said the pancake...

and it hitched a ride
on a kite to escape the fox.

It landed at the edge of a forest. By the forest was a pig in a pen.

Now the pig wanted to eat the pancake too, but he was too clever to say so.

"What's the hurry, Mr. Pancake?" he asked. "Let me walk through the forest with you. It's a dangerous place."

The pancake looked into the forest. Maybe the pig was right.

"Quickly!" he gasped. "Don't let them catch me!"

"What did you say?" asked the pig.

"I SAID, DON'T LET THEM CATCH ME!" shouted the pancake.

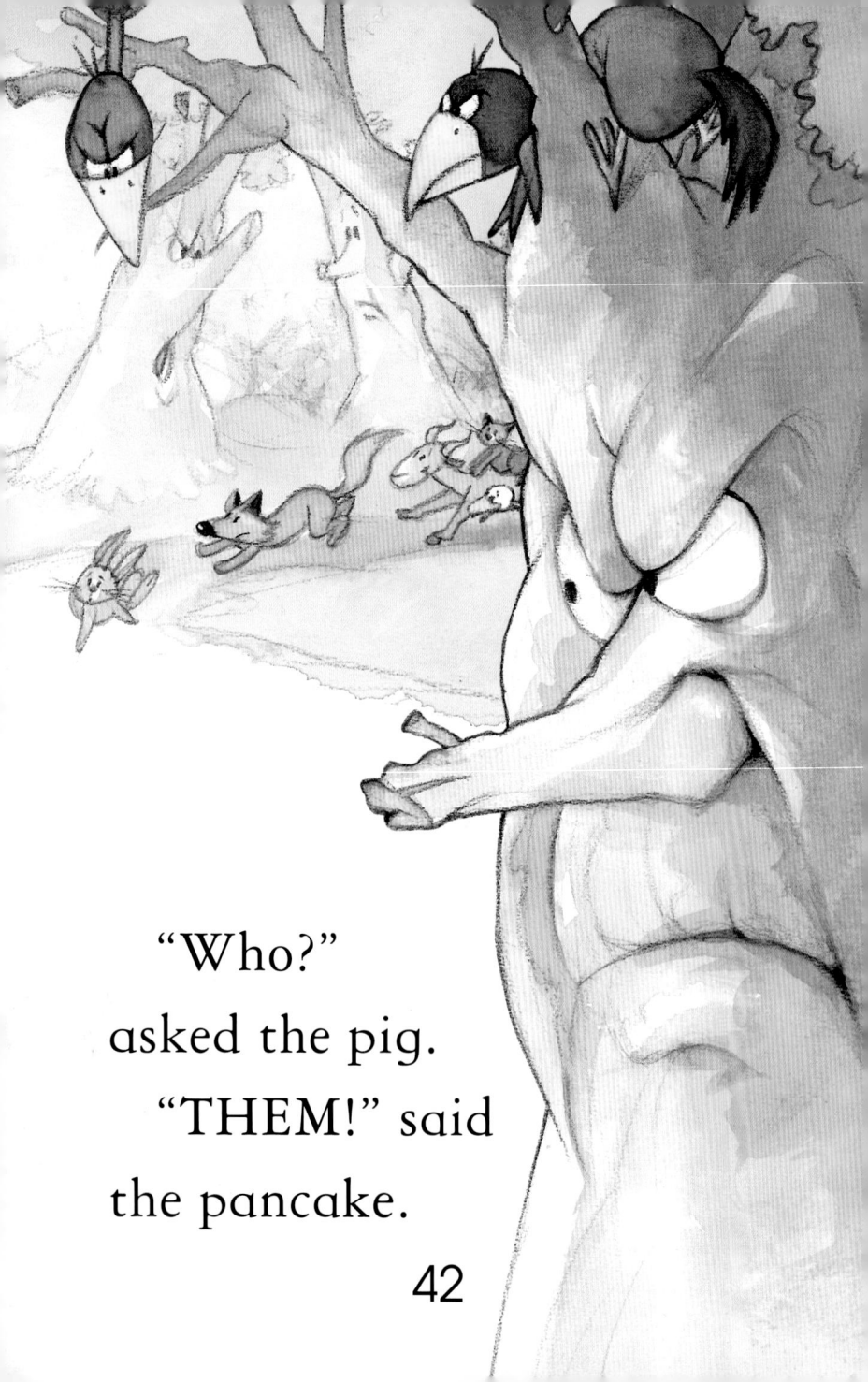

"Who?"
asked the pig.
"THEM!" said
the pancake.

"The fox, the goat, the cat, the duck, the rabbit, the dog and all the family."
Look, right there!

"I'm sorry," said the pig. "I can't hear you. You'll have to come closer."

The pancake jumped over the fence and into the pen.

"I SAID, THE FOX, THE GOAT," the pancake began.

But before he could shout any more, the pig snapped him up and swallowed him...

...in one gulp.

*The Runaway Pancake* is a folk tale from Germany and Norway. There are different versions with different characters, but the pancake always gets eaten at the end.

Series editor:
Lesley Sims

Designed by
Russell Punter and Louise Flutter

First published in 2006 by Usborne Publishing Ltd., Usborne House, 83-85 Saffron Hill, London EC1N 8RT, England. www.usborne.com
Copyright © 2006 Usborne Publishing Ltd.

All rights reserved. No part of this publication may be reproduced, stored in a retrieval system or transmitted in any form or by any means, electronic, mechanical, photocopying, recording or otherwise without the prior permission of the publisher. The name Usborne and the devices are Trade Marks of Usborne Publishing Ltd.
Printed in China. UE. First published in America in 2006.

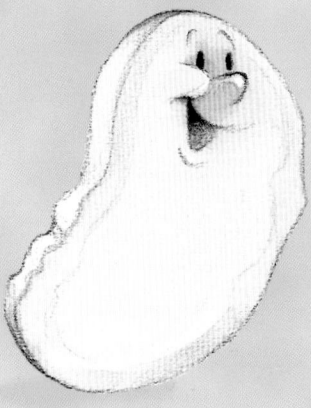